For Robin Tzannes, friend and flea expert
K.P.

www.korkypaul.com

For Roo
P.R.

A Bodley Head Book: 0 370 32632 6

First published in 2002 in Great Britain by The Bodley Head,
an imprint of Random House Children's Books

1 3 5 7 9 10 8 6 4 2

Text copyright © Paul Rogers 2002
Illustrations copyright © Korky Paul 2002

RANDOM HOUSE CHILDREN'S BOOKS
61-63 Uxbridge Road, London W5 5SA,
A division of The Random House Group, Ltd.

RANDOM HOUSE AUSTRALIA (PTY) LTD
20 Alfred Street, Milsons Point, Sydney,
New South Wales 2061, Australia

RANDOM HOUSE NEW ZEALAND LTD
18 Poland Road, Glenfield, Auckland 10, New Zealand

RANDOM HOUSE (PTY) LTD
Endulini, 5A Jubilee Road, Parktown 2193, South Africa

THE RANDOM HOUSE GROUP Limited Reg. No. 954009
www.randomhouse.co.uk

A CIP catalogue record for this book is available from the British Library.

Printed and bound in Singapore

Paul Rogers & Korky Paul

Tiny

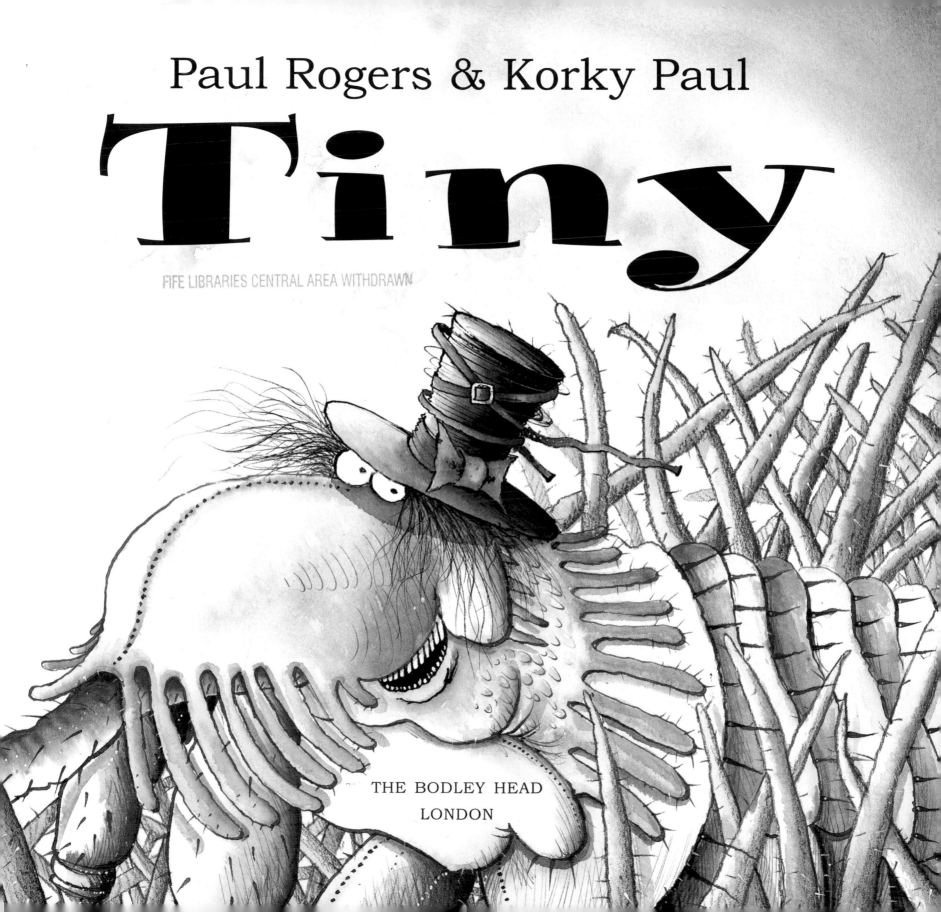

THE BODLEY HEAD

LONDON

Once upon a time there was a flea called Tiny.

And the flea lived on a dog

called Cleopatra.

72

And the dog lived
at a house
called number
seventy-two.

And the house was in a road

called Hilltop Road.

And the road was in a town

called Remembrance.

And the town was on an island

called Great Hope.

And the island was in the ocean on a planet

called Earth.

And the Earth was in a sort of heavenly merry-go-round

Jupiter

Mars

Earth

Venus

Mercury

called the solar system.

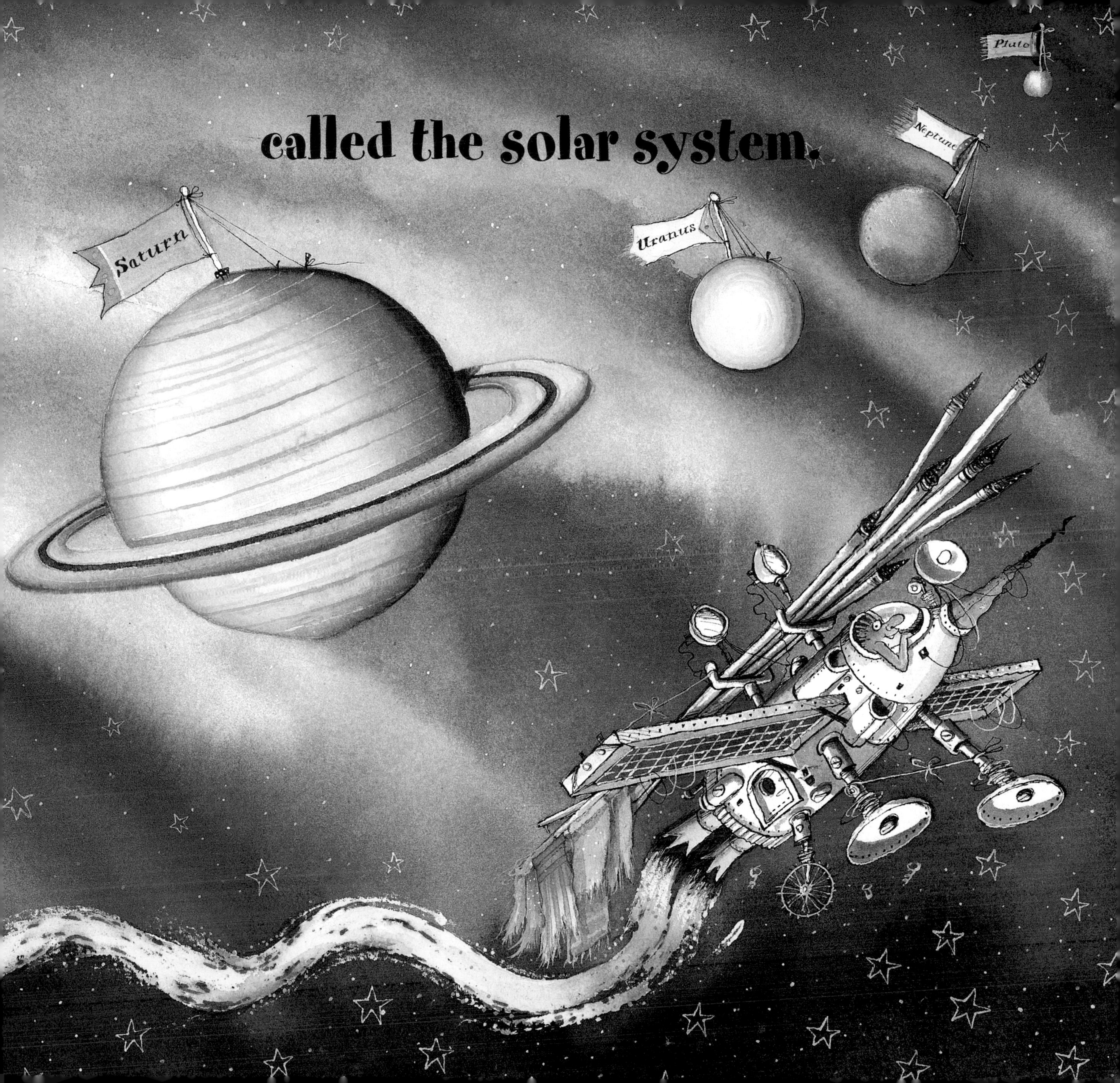

And the solar system was in a galaxy

full of huge stars far bigger than the sun.

And one evening Cleopatra had a jolly good scratch and
Tiny fell off and landed on his back.

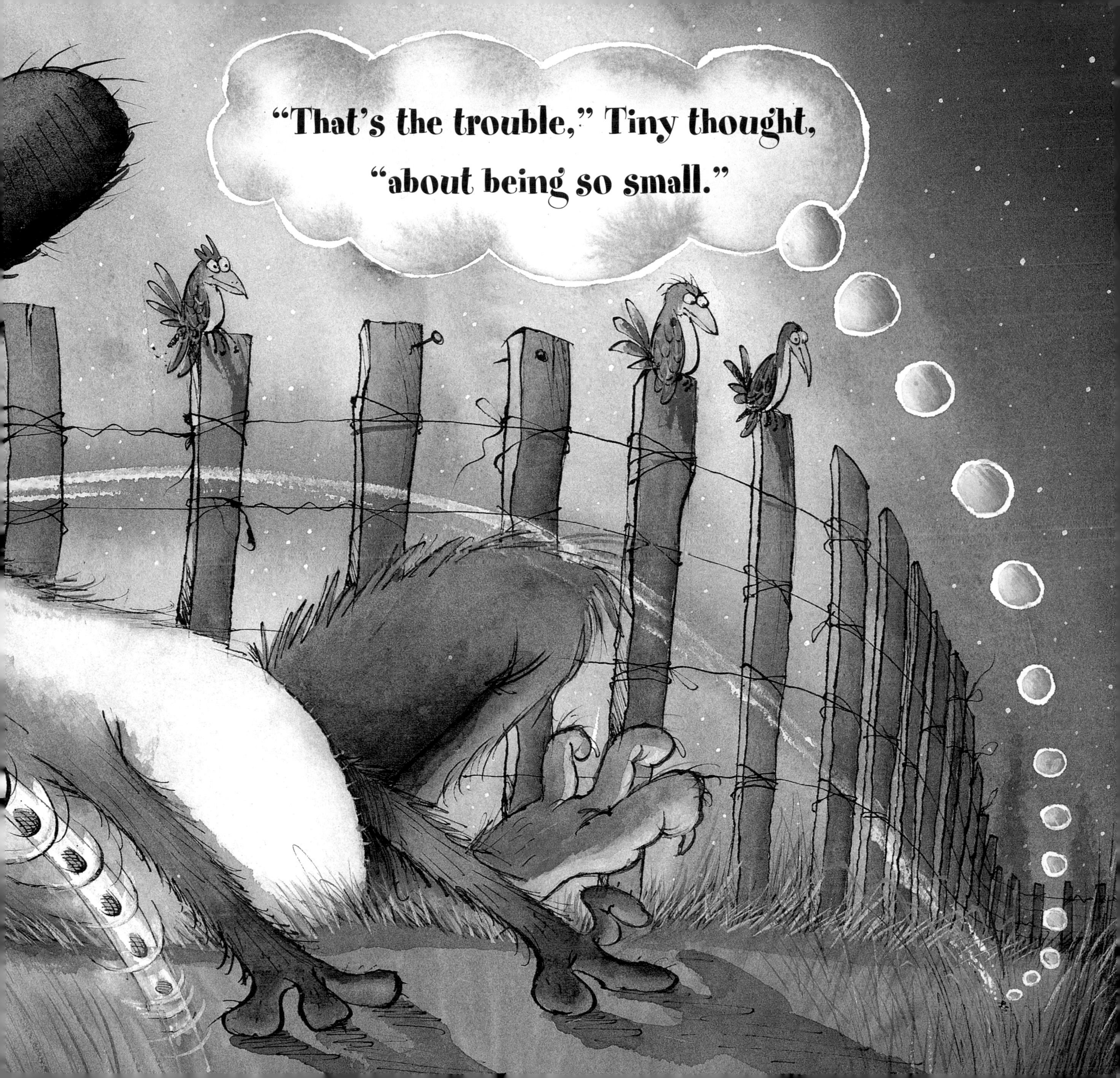
"That's the trouble," Tiny thought, "about being so small."

Then he looked up, and for the first time in his life he saw the stars.
"Good heavens!" he thought. "Some of them are even tinier than me!"

"Perhaps it doesn't matter that I'm so small after all."

And thinking that happy thought, he sat there waiting...

...until the next dog came along.

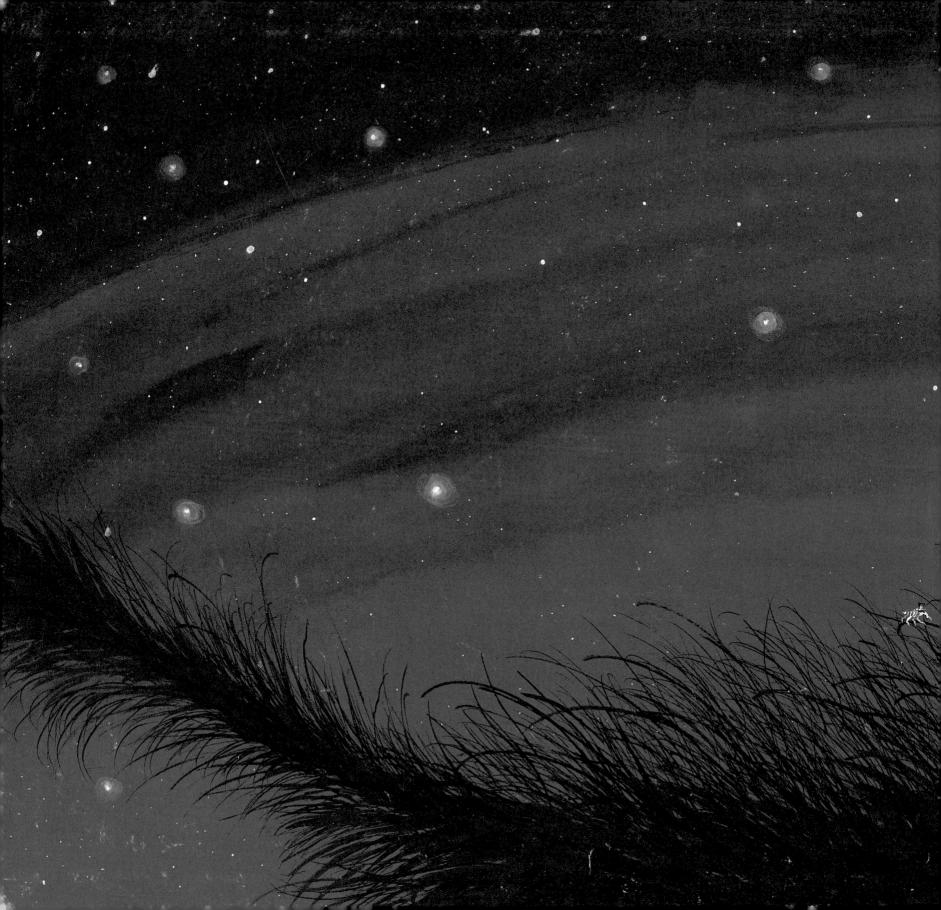